Fuel of Life

Luis M. Cruz

Published by Dark Fire Press LLC

Cover & Interior Illustrations by Angel M. Martinez

ISBN Paperback: 978-1-7346365-1-2
ISBN Digital: 978-1-7346365-3-6

www.darkfirepress.com

First Edition: October 2020

CREATOR & WRITER:

Luis M. Cruz

ARTIST:

Angel M. Martinez

Published by Dark Fire Press
New Jersey, USA

urner orbits Earth several times, before landing the ship on Central Park, New York, near the Dakota building. It's a little past midnight, as she exits the ship, takes a few steps and falls to her knees on the grass looking up at the beautiful night sky. never giving a thought to how lovely this warm spring night air feels.

"This is incredible." Turner muttered as she looked around.

"Why. Did you think we would destroy ourselves?" Asked a voice from a man who stood behind the ship, "Forgive me, my name is Antonio Carro."

"I'm Elizabeth Turner." She said while getting up from the ground.

"Military, from what I can tell by your clothing and, is that blood?"

"Yes."

Antonio walks towards her while passing his hand against the ships steel hull,

"So what brings you back, other than the ship I mean." "It's a long story."

"The night is young."

Turner sits on the grass and begins to tell him what happened,

"I guess it all began when we detected the oncoming asteroid..."

The past

Within hours, every nations leader met in the neutral country of Switzerland. It's the first time in history the government leaders had all came to one decision, to keep the information of the asteroid from the public, at least until a confirmation of the was made.

During the following years, thousands of newly designed space shuttles were built, much larger than its predecessor, but the most significant change happened two years after the confirmation of the asteroid, the unification of Earth's countries. As a result of the unity on Earth, the asteroid transmitted the codes required to shut down the shield. Certain laws were also passed, that of course, the people had the right to vote for.

There was one law in which the people could not vote for or against, no matter how inhumane it sounded. The law stated that anyone who has committed a crime, i.e., murder, would remain on Earth and die with it. Everyone, even the prisoners themselves, considered the law to be harsh and cruel.

Eight years passed, and humans during the time have become accustomed to the living accommodations of the asteroid, which was really about the size of the Earth's moon. However it wasn't as round as the moon, it had more of an oval egg shape. The inside of the asteroid was very technologically advanced than anything the human race had ever seen or thought of. The surface of the asteroid was made of rock, but the interior was constructed of steel.

A new government is quickly established, calling itself the U.H.E. (United Humans of Earth,) this new government was formed much like that of the former United States. The aliens that designed this asteroid thought of everything, they knew the humans would need to travel from one side of the asteroid to the other. They built tunnels that resembled subway tunnels, except for the trains.

FUEL OF LIFE

However, there were small, elevator like, cabins that would take a person completely around the asteroid in three minutes. What people found most incredible about the cabins was that no one felt the speed of it, and nobody could figure out how many each tunnel contained. Just as the people from Earth were getting comfortable living on the asteroid, human bodies were being discovered dead. Every body that was found, whether adult or infant, was drained of his or her blood. The victims had three puncture wounds, one on the neck and the other two were on both the right and left wrists of the bodies. At first the authorities thought that there was a criminal on the loose committing the crimes, but that was quickly dismissed seeing as how there were fifty to a hundred people being killed a day. The authorities were ordered to search the asteroid thoroughly and cautiously, inside and out. The authorities, since the arrival to the asteroid, were always working as one unit but divided into several platoons.

One of these platoons is dispatched to search the upper north section of the asteroid, and each soldier from the platoon had order's to split-up and search the perimeter. One soldier, a female, suddenly came across an odd looking door, at the end of a long corridor. The door wasn't on any of the schematics the aliens had provided, it was four stories high and thirty-five yards wide, it looked like an oversized garage door.

The soldier, before entering, radio's her commanding officer who was several hundred yards away, "Private Turner to Colonel Claremont, come in sir." "Colonel Claremont here."

FUEL OF LIFE

He responded while looking in her direction. "Sir." She said nervous-
ly, "I think you should come and see this." "What is it?" "It's some
kind of door, a really large door." "Whatever you do, don't touch it.
I'm on my way." As Col. Claremont ran down the corridor toward
Private Turner he ordered the rest of the platoon, which were scattered throughout the perimeter, to converge on her location.

As Private Turner stood by the door, she heard a noise coming from
inside. It was a loud banging sound, as if a sack of potatoes were
being dropped to the ground continuously. The young, inexperien-
ced, female soldier quickly stood in front of the door pointing her
machine gun at it. The banging sound suddenly stopped, the door is
once again silent, at least that's what she thought.

Not a minute has passed and yet again a sound is heard from the door,
this time it wasn't a banging sound. It was now a low scratching
sound, as if though someone or something was rubbing its nails up
and down the steel door, trying to lure her inside. Private Turner
becomes impatient, and begins to take small, nervous-like, steps
towards the door. When she got close enough, she reached, with one
hand, for the control panel attached to the door that she assumed
would open it, while holding the machine gun in the other. The sound
seemed to get louder with every heartbeat and, just when she was
about to touch one of the buttons on the control panel, she heard
footsteps. At least a dozen, or more, running towards her.

Turner quickly takes a few steps back and again held her machine gun with both hands before her commanding officer noticed. The entire platoon was now by the large door, ready to shoot anyone or anything that came out of it.

"Report Private." He ordered, as he stood alongside of her.

"I came across the door while searching the perimeter, and noticed that it wasn't on the schematics the aliens left for us. But that's not all, after I contacted you I heard a noise coming from inside the door."

"What kind of noise?"

"At first it was banging sounds, then it changed into a sort of scratching." "Everyone, stand ready." He ordered, walking to the control panel, which was located on the center of the door and entered the standard command code.

The door slid open just like a garage door, but it was too dark to see inside.

The soldiers quickly turned on their helmet and machine gun flashlights, and were now able to see steps on the right hand side of the door leading downward to a lower level. "Everybody follow me, but be careful and stay alert." Warned Col. Claremont, as he lead the platoon down the stairs.

It took them forty-five minutes to reach the bottom. Immediately after all the soldiers stepped off the last step of the stairs, the flashlights from both the helmets and machine guns shut off, leaving everyone in the dark for a few seconds. Suddenly the lights come on, not from the flashlights, but from inside the area.

The area stretched out for miles, none of the soldiers were able to see the end of the place. It didn't matter which way they looked, they could not see any other wall only the one behind them. Alongside the soldiers, were rows of glass barrel-like vats, that extended as far as the eye can see. Each vat was seventeen stories high, and fifty feet wide in diameter.

They were filled with red liquid, some were filled to the top, others only halfway. As the soldiers walked by the vats, row after row, they didn't notice or heard what was closing in from behind, preventing them from retreating back to the stairs. Once the soldiers were surrounded, the aliens made themselves noticeable with a screeching almost growling sound. The soldiers, in a frantic, quickly pointed their M-16's at them, but did not have time to react. As soon as they turned, the aliens which looked human, attacked, quickly puncturing three holes on each of the soldiers' arms, draining them of their blood.

The puncture wounds were made by tentacles which extended from the aliens right and left index fingers into the victims wrist veins. The third wound is on the victims neck, which is caused from their forked tongue. Some of the soldiers tried to escape, but failed after getting so close. After draining the blood from a human body, they would fly to the top of the vats and regurgitate the blood into them. Col. Claremont, witnessing nearly all of his troops die, headed passed them to the stairs.

FUEL OF LIFE

He was the only one to make it to the top, before stumbling just a few feet away from the door, out of breath, desperately gasping for air. Suddenly a pair of black leather boots stands before him, he looks up and although he was exhausted from running up the stairs, he managed to utter one word, "Why?"

The alien who stood before him kept silent for a couple of seconds, as if deciding whether or not the Colonel deserved an explanation. The alien instead dropped to his knees, punctured three holes, and began to drain his blood.

Private Turner put up a hell of a struggle than most of the more experienced soldiers. She used her M-16 machine gun till it was out of ammo, she then reached for her standard issued side arm pistol, while simultaneously rolling herself on the floor and grabbing another handgun from a fallen soldier. She did fine for about two minutes, till they also ran out of bullets. The soldiers were trained in mainly martial arts, which also worked for her, but the aliens were overwhelming. From out of nowhere one of the aliens swooped down, hoisted her by the throat, lifting her up several yards from the ground. The alien had a helmet and vest that belonged to one of the soldiers over his own clothing, which was comprised of leather.

Desperately she tried to gasp for air, but the grip he had on her throat prevented her from doing much. Turner would throw punches at the aliens' ribcage, but becoming weaker with every punch. She then gave the alien a swift kick to the groin, causing the alien to release his grip and drop her.

FUEL OF LIFE

She landed inside one of the blood filled vats in which she quickly surfaced and wanted to come out, but she was winded. As disgusted as she was feeling from being in the pool of blood, she knew that if she climbed out, she would be killed.

She felt horrified watching her friends and teammates get slaughtered by the aliens, even more so when she realized how naturally warm the blood she floated on was, although she could have done without the copper-like odor. She observed as the aliens piled the dead bodies near some of the vats, including the one she was in.

"Now that these soldiers are dead, we must go out and rid ourselves of these infestations!" Shouted an alien from on top of the stairwell. He had long black shoulder length hair, as did all of them whether male or female, although their hair color differed.

"This one must be the leader." Turner thought. Though she couldn't do anything, except hide deeper in the pool of blood as she watched them take flight like a swarm of bees. Once they departed she climbed out from the vat and landed on the pile of corpse's, to soften her fall. Her hair, which was in a ponytail and stuffed in the helmet at the beginning of the mission, was no longer blonde. It was loose, drenched wet from the pool of blood, and had an almost eerie red look to it.

After changing her clothes with another soldier, who was similar in size, she gathered weapons and grabbed a backpack full extra ammunition. Turner went to every pile of corpse, where she either climbed or sifted through them, to retrieve their dog tags and put them in her backpack.

FUEL OF LIFE

Since she didn't find Col. Claremont's body to retrieve his dog tag, she smiled with the thought that perhaps he escaped and is hiding somewhere in the asteroid. When she reaches the top of the stairwell and approaches the door, she hears a mumbling sound which sounded like someone struggling to talk. Taking her handgun from under her arm, she begins to carefully go through the door where she hears a slurping sound.

Private Turner witnesses an alien creature kneeled down beside a soldiers body, feeding. Trying not to make a sound, she walks right up behind the kneeled creature and points her handgun directly in the back of its head. Ever so gently, she begins to pull on the trigger when suddenly the creature stands up from the floor and faces her.

"Holy-sh--" She said, as the alien knocks the gun from her hand and grabs her by the throat, lifting her a few inches from the floor and slamming her against the wall on the side of the door.

The creature growled as he tightened his grip on her throat, "you need a mint." She managed to say as she grabbed the gun from her thigh and shot the alien creature on the crotch, causing him to release his grip. The creature yells out a loud, horrible scream, as he dropped to one knee in agony. She aims her gun to his head and shoots him, point blank, in the forehead. Her face, sprayed with the blood of the creature, her body, writhing with pain and exhaustion, walks toward the body from which the alien was feeding and was surprised to find that it was Col. Claremont, barely breathing.

"Colonel, it's alright. We're gonna make it outta here." She said, trying to prevent him from bleeding to death by applying pressure to the opened wounds.

"Too late... For me..." The Colonel's voice was low, his breathing was heavy and was coughing up blood, "Save yourself..."

"No, we'll get out of here together."

"No!" He yelled, before choking from his own blood.

"But why?"

"Plan... To kill everybody onboard... By draining our blood... For fuel... To orbit Earth... Where they will... Do the same to the people... We left behind... For many generations..." He then took one final breath and died.

Turner gently removes his dog tag from around his neck, places it in her backpack with the rest of them. Arriving at the populated area of the asteroid, she was horrified to find thousands of dead, mutilated, bodies of men, women and children everywhere. Most of the bodies were missing limbs, which were scattered everywhere. As she walked toward the launch-bay, passing body after body, there were creatures still feeding on humans. She felt helpless that she couldn't do anything but keep walking. People screamed for help, but would quickly be silenced by the creatures hunger. Some would reach out for her by grabbing her legs or ankles, while others grabbed and miss. She was now just several yards away from the launch-bay doors, where she could clearly see the front end of a ship.

"Where do you think you're going?" uttered a female creature who now stood in her way, dripping of blood from her mouth, wearing a bulletproof military vest. Turner just stopped and remained quiet, not looking directly at the creatures face so as not to be recognized for a human.

"I will not ask again." The female creature said, as she walked closer and looked at Turner from head to toe, "And why do you carry these human weapons?"

"They are souvenirs, like the vest you have on, from the victims I have slaughtered." Turner answered, looking at her up and down and feeling angry for saying what she said instead of just killing her where she stood, "And I'm going to check if there are any survivors in the launch-bay, for I still hunger."

Turner then proceeded toward the launch-bay, as the female creature stepped aside she took a sniff of her, "Your scent."

"What about it?"

"It smells like you have already feasted."

"Perhaps I did. Why does it concern you?"

"It does not."

"Very well then." Turner muttered as she continued to walk toward the launch-bay.

"But what does concern me is that your scent stinks like human."

Turner didn't have time to face her again, the female creature had already thrown herself on Turner, catching her on the back of her neck, knocking both of them to the cold steel floor. The creature quickly turns her around and gives her one good punch on the face, nearly knocking Turner unconscious. Noticing that the creature had her mouth open, and was most likely about to kill her. Turner to reached for one of her guns, puts it into the creatures mouth and pulls the trigger, blasting her alien brain from its skull. That got the attention of every bloodsucking creature in the area, which she figured was at least a thousand or more.

She quickly gets up from the floor and makes a run for the launch-bay, all the while shooting at every bloodsucking creature that got in her way. Turner knows that as long as she keeps running, she won't have time to reload her guns, so she made every shot count. When a gun ran out of ammo, she would drop it or throw it at the creatures to distract them while she reached for another gun. It was one long straightaway between her and the launch-bay, she was now down to one gun as she finally makes it inside, with a quick glance around she realizes that all the shuttles were either missing parts or dismantled. Running toward the control panel that closes the launch-bay doors, she fires her last five bullets, shooting the targets all in the forehead.

Before the doors shut, three bloodsucking creatures manage to get in. She pulls out a bowie survival knife while running to every shuttle trying to find a way to escape off the rock. Suddenly one of the creatures, a red haired female, tackled her to the ground, knocking the knife from her hand.

FUEL OF LIFE

The creature smacks Turner to the floor so hard that it knocked a tooth out. Turner clenched her fist and punches the creature on the side of the head, near the temple, causing the creature to become disoriented. Then grabbing a screwdriver, she plunges it into the creatures eye socket. The creature screams in pain, while pulling the screwdriver out. Seeing an opportunity to make a run for her knife, a male creature quickly steps on it, while another male creature grabs her from behind in a chokehold.

"I have her!" The creature yelled.

"Good," She said, as she licked the blood from the screwdriver and watching as her victim tried to escape. "Keep her still while I do the same to her."

The creature grabs Turner by her cheeks, while the other two bloodsuckers struggle to hold her body from moving. "Now you shall see with one eye, as I pluck the other from your socket and eat it, before your flesh is ripped apart by them."

The creature lets out a grunt as she begins to plunge the screwdriver towards Turners head, but misses and instead impales it into the throat of the creature that held her from behind. Somehow Turner found the strength to dodge her, and release herself from their grip. The female bloodsucker didn't care that she just killed one of her own people, she simply pulled the screwdriver out from his throat just as easily as she lunged it in. As the impaled creature falls, Turner grabs the knife from the floor and stabs the other creature above the groin. Then she twists the knife and moves it upward, causing

FUEL OF LIFE

the creatures entrails to drop to the floor while still standing. She then pulls the knife out, and shoves it through the bottom of the female bloodsuckers' chin.

She sits beside the dead body, resting and listening to the mob of bloodsucking creatures banging at the door trying to get inside. It wouldn't be long before the creatures knock the door down and kill her, so she gets up from the floor and begins to walk around the launch-bay, looking very closely at the dismantled ships, trying to figure out which one to harvest for parts. She comes across a ship that she's never seen Before, and quickly realized that the ship wasn't designed by a human.

The ship hovered about one foot off the floor, it had a black metallic color with a red line trimmed across from bow to stern and its design resembled a boomerang. The entrance to the cockpit was located above the ship where the two wings merged. The cockpit was designed for one pilot, with a limited cargo space. It took her a few minutes to figure out the navigational systems, and why they kept shutting off. She assumed the ship was lacking one important thing, fuel. She notices a vat, not as large as the ones she seen before, but still large enough to hold quit a few gallons of blood. The vat had a transparent hose that was attached to the rear, right side, of the ship and next to the vat was a control console.

The activation of the console projected a holographic keypad, however, she could not understand the markings. The hordes of creatures were on the verge of breaking down the door, she begins to randomly touch every button, in the hope that one will start the machine.

Suddenly, a loud hum is heard, and the vat begins to pump blood through the hose and into the ship. After a few minutes, the console shuts the vat off. Turner hoped that it meant the fuel tank had enough to get her back to Earth. Just as the aliens forced themselves inside the launch-bay like a swarm of ants, she disconnected the hose and quickly boarded the ship.

The ships door closed, as two creatures almost boarded. The launch-bay departure doors were closed, she wasn't sure whether the control console she used to fuel the ship would have also been the controls to open them but she would rather die trying to escape, than to die by the hands of the creatures. The ship lifts off toward the closed doors. Turner begins to say a little prayer, but before she can finish, the doors open and allows the ship to depart into open space toward Earth.

Present.

"It only took thirty minutes to get back." She said as she got up from the ground, "How did Earth's survivors manage?"

"It was a little rough in the beginning but, as you can see, we did alright." He replied, "What about you, what will you do now?"

"I'm goin' to warn the people." She said, admiring the night sky.

"I'm sorry. But I can't let you do that."

"What!?!" By the time she turned around, it was too late. Antonio was alreadybehind her with his tentacles and forked tongue exposed, and before she could blink, he was already draining her blood. He drained her slowly, as he laid her body gently on the grass.

FUEL OF LIFE

"I need you." He told her, "Actually, just your blood to fuel this ship so that I can rejoin my kind. My people and I were stranded on this planet for centuries, everyday was a struggle for survival. We were pushed to extinction by your kind. Feeding became more difficult with every century that passed, I was captured after feasting and was branded a serial killer one month before your kind left the criminals to die. I was charged with murder, but I had to eat. Now, thanks to you, I have transportation and you for fuel. However, I can't let you warn your people. We will use your people the way you use cattle, we're going to feed upon your kind whenever necessary." He then punctured her neck with his tongue, and finished draining her body of blood. Once done he went to the rear side of the ship, placed his mouth on the nozzle and regurgitated the blood.

He then dragged Turner's body into the small cargo area of the ship and said, "I'm taking you in case I get hungry." Although she was dead, he felt the need to talk to her.

After dragging her lifeless body inside the ship, he grabbed a pouch that contained the dog tags from her fallen platoon, and tossed it out the door. Before flying off he walked to the cargo area, grabbed her body and dragged it back off. He dug a hole in the grass several yards away from the ship, with his bare hands and placed her body there, along with the dog tags and covered the hole.

He doesn't know why he did that, was it out of compassion or the fact that certain human characteristics had somehow rubbed off on him. He boards the ship as dawn approaches, and takes off for the asteroid. Centuries passed, people were reported missing or found dead with puncture wounds. Humanity thought nothing of it, after all, for centuries people were always reported missing or dead. As for the puncture wounds, some people thought it was the Chupacabra. Not once did the survivors of Earth think that the inhabitants from the asteroid were the cause, they weren't even aware that life existed in the asteroid other than humans. They were too busy thanking God, or a higher being, for saving Earth and their lives...

THE END...

FUEL OF LIFE

GORY SKETCHES

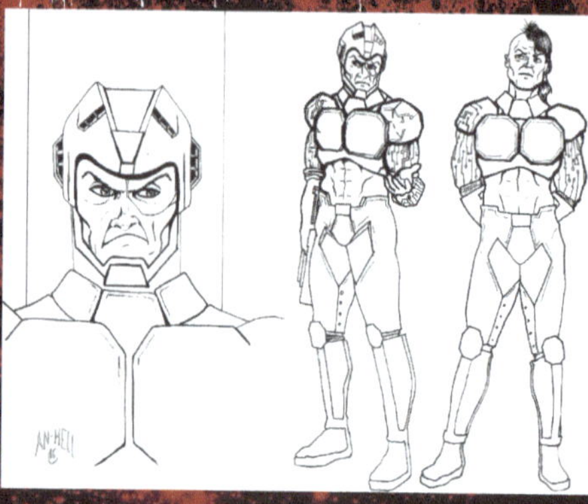

The original design of the suits was made by Luis M. Cruz, I based on these designs and made a mix between the Marvel´s character "Valkyrie" (for Turner) and "Marters of the universe" character "Man-at-arms ".

During the illustrations, we received the news of the death of Prince, I asked Luis if we could pay tribute to this wonderful artist, putting his facial features in the character Antonio Carro, Luis agreed.

BIO:

I Am A Writer. Therefore, I Am Not Sane."
—Edgar Allen Poe

Luis M. Cruz has Arthrogryposis, which is Latin for curvature of the joints and muscles, but that doesn't stop him from following his dreams. Luis is not only the Author of the YA science fiction/horror book FUEL OF LIFE: An Illustrated Novel, he's also the Author of the YA science fiction novel, THE DAY THEY MADE CONTACT. He is also the publisher of CRUZIN-COMICS and Creator/Writer of JENNIFER THE SHE-WOLF, BLOOD-KILL, A.L.F.A., as well as THE WORKOUT - Erotica From A Handicaps P.O.V.: An Illustrated novel. All of which are available on Amazon and, Indy-Planet. While Luis loves to read and write comic books his passion, however, is reading and writing Science Fiction, Fantasy and a little Horror.

BIO:

I'm **Angel M. Martínez** (Ammardi) Artist for **CRUZINCOMICS** of BLOOD-KILL and FUEL OF LIFE.
My creative beginnings date from 1987 (It's a long story), in 2012 I contact with Gene Tipton, and I start drawing and inking comic "Into the Basement" for Shoot in the Dark comics. At the same time, i also came into contact with R- Comics , with whom I made the short story "It Should be painted red" and subsequently the "New Dawn." In 2013 I contact ed Isaac D. Quattlebaun, which i worked on "Wicked is the new black", "Husk" and recently "Loomis Valley Mysteries" series. In 2015 i made contact with **Luis M. Cruz**, publisher of **Cruzin Comics**, New York, for whom I began to drawing two series, "Blood Kill" and "Target". Continued with literary illustration collaborating with Tery Logan (Beatriz Tante), for a cover design and illustration for the book "Tales of a Logan". The creative chemistry between us formed tandem for future projects, the most immediate, adaptation to comic book story written by Tery Logan entitled "Blood and Wings".
Recently he has written and drawn a comic called "La Luna de Ferror" for the magazine "Mundo Masters".